Yankee Stadium is located in The Bronx, one of the five boroughs of New York City.

The *New York Yankees* were preparing for the start of a new baseball season. The team had just returned to New York from their *Spring Training* home in Florida. Back at *Yankee Stadium*, the *Bronx Bombers* were taking batting practice. All eyes were on the team's young star, a rookie named Robbie. Robbie's teammates nicknamed him "Robbie the Rookie." Other Yankees players looked on as Robbie hit baseballs into the stands. "Nice hit, Robbie the Rookie!" said the players, as they watched in amazement.

With Opening Day just a day away, Robbie the Rookie decided to explore *Yankees* Town after practice. Robbie grabbed his camera and map as he left the ballpark. Yankees fans nearby waved and said, "Have a great trip, Robbie the Rookie!"

An estimated 14,000 taxicabs service New York City.

Robbie was excited to finally have the opportunity to see Yankees Town. He hailed a cab outside the ballpark and instructed the driver to take him to his first stop, The Bronx Zoo.

At the zoo, Robbie saw many amazing animals and learned a lot about their habitats. His favorite exhibit was the Monkey House, where a chimp immediately recognized the young Yankees ballplayer and called, "Hello, Robbie the Rookie!" Robbie waved and called back, "Let's go, Yankees!"

The Bronx Zoo is the largest zoo in the United States and is home to more than 4,000 animals.

Long Island is the largest island in the continental United States and is home to over seven million people.

Robbie headed out to Long Island. At Montauk Beach, he built an amazing sand castle with young Yankees fans. He also flew a kite high above the sand. The children cheered, "Let's go, Yankees!"

Montauk Lighthouse, standing over 100 feet tall, was completed in 1796 and is located on the eastern tip of Long Island.

Next, it was on to the eastern tip of Long Island and Montauk Lighthouse. Robbie posed for pictures with Yankees fans in front of the lighthouse. He climbed all the way to the top and looked out over the vast Atlantic Ocean. Seagulls flying overhead noticed his pinstripes and squawked, "Hello, Robbie the Rookie!"

Built in 1927, Coney Island's Cyclone roller coaster is one of the oldest wooden roller coasters in America.

Ready for some thrills, Robbie the Rookie was off to an amusement park on Coney Island. His first stop was the ice cream shop, where he ordered a double scoop of his favorite flavor – blueberry bubblegum. As Robbie gobbled up the treat, he made a mess all over his face and uniform!

With no time to waste, Robbie stood in line for the world-famous Cyclone roller coaster. He rode in the first car as the coaster twisted, turned, dipped, and looped. Everyone aboard screamed with excitement. Yankees fans called, "Hold on to your hat, Robbie!"

The Brooklyn Bridge spans the East River, connecting Manhattan to Brooklyn, and was completed in 1873.

Two of New York's most famous neighborhoods are Little Italy and Chinatown, both on the island of Manhattan.

Robbie the Rookie walked across the Brooklyn Bridge as he made his way to Manhattan. He passed walkers, joggers, and many sightseers. Everywhere he went, Robbie was greeted by fans. They cheered, "Hello, Robbie the Rookie!"

In Manhattan, Robbie explored some of the city's most famous neighborhoods. In Chinatown, he arrived just in time for a parade. A dragon wound through Chinatown as large crowds lined the streets. A voice from inside the dragon called, "Ni hao, Robbie the Rookie"

Robbie then went to Little Italy. He learned to toss pizza dough high in the air. A young Yankees fan was excited to see the ballplayer in the restaurant. The boy cheered, "Salve, Robbie the Rookie!"

The Statue of Liberty, located on Liberty Island in the Hudson River, stands 151 feet, 1 inch, from base to torch.

The Statue of Liberty was a gift to the United States by the people of France in 1886.

Robbie boarded a ferry bound for the Statue of Liberty. He posed for pictures with a new friend and learned a lot about the monument. Noticing Robbie, tourists from all over the world called, "Hello, Robbie the Rookie!"

Wanting to get a closer look, Robbie and several of his new friends climbed to Lady Liberty's crown and enjoyed spectacular views of New York. Visiting the Statue of Liberty made Robbie proud to be an American.

The Empire State Building was once the tallest building in the world, standing 102 stories tall and 1,472 feet from the ground to the top of its spire.

Robbie the Rookie took a ferry back to Manhattan and headed uptown, stopping at the Empire State Building. He was amazed at how tall the skyscraper was!

Instead of riding an elevator, Robbie took the stairs all the way to the observation deck. From the eighty-sixth floor, Robbie the Rookie looked out over Yankees Town in all directions.

There are 1,576 steps from the ground level to the 86th floor observation deck of the Empire State Building.

From the Empire State Building, it was on to another famous midtown landmark: Rockefeller Center. Once there, Robbie reluctantly agreed to rent skates and try his luck at ice-skating.

Rockefeller Center's skating rink opened on Christmas Day, 1936, and is considered the most famous ice rink in the world. The rink is open from October to April.

Robbie never imagined that keeping his balance would be so difficult. He fell on the ice time after time, while youngsters whizzed by him. The children teased, "Whoa, Robbie the Rookie!"

Happy to get off his skates, Robbie was ready for a sport he was more comfortable with – baseball! He played catch in the park with a new friend. "Catch, Robbie!" the girl said, as she delivered a fastball.

Central Park is a favorite destination for New Yorkers and tourists, making it the most visited park in the United States.

Next, he raced remote control boats at a Central Park pond. Everywhere he went, he was greeted by adoring Yankees fans cheering, "Hello, Robbie the Rookie!"

The Metropolitan Museum of Art opened in 1872 and is one of the largest art galleries in the world.

From Central Park, Robbie made the short walk to the Metropolitan Museum of Art. At the Met, the friendly ballplayer roamed the exhibit halls and appreciated various forms of art. He saw exhibits from all over the world. Spending time at the museum gave Robbie some ideas for an art project he wanted to work on!

The New York City Subway, with its 468 stations and 842 miles of tracks, is one of the busiest subway systems in the world.

Robbie took the subway from the Met down to Times Square. All this traveling sure made him hungry. Fortunately, he walked right by a street vendor and picked up a delicious snack. The street vendor recognized the ballplayer and called, "Hello, Robbie the Rookie!"

As day turned to night, Robbie found himself in the heart of Times Square. The crowded sidewalks and the dazzling lights made Times Square such an exciting place to be. Surprised to see the baseball player, fans cheered, "Hello, Robbie the Rookie!"

There are approximately 12,000 street vendors in New York City.

Times Square is the symbolic center of New York City and annually hosts the most famous New Year's Eve countdown in the world.

After a full day of sightseeing, Robbie the Rookie finally made it back to his house near Yankee Stadium. He comfortably rested on his recliner and reflected on all the interesting places he had visited and the nice people he ran into along the way. He was happy to be a member of the New York Yankees and couldn't wait for the season to begin.

As Robbie the Rookie drifted off to sleep, he thought, "I love New York!"

For Anna and Maya. ~ Aimee Aryal

For Ang and Ben. ~ Brad V

For more information about our products,
please visit us online at www.mascotbooks.com.

Copyright © 2008, Mascot Books, Inc. All rights reserved.
No part of this book may be reproduced by any means.

Mascot Books, Inc.
P.O. Box 220157
Chantilly, VA 20153-0157

Major League Baseball trademarks and copyrights are used
with permission of Major League Baseball Properties, Inc.

ISBN: 1-932888-76-4

Printed in the United States.

www.mascotbooks.com

Title List

Major League Baseball

Boston Red Sox	Hello, *Wally*!	Jerry Remy
Boston Red Sox	*Wally The Green Monster* And His Journey Through *Red Sox Nation*!	Jerry Remy
Boston Red Sox	Coast to Coast with *Wally The Green Monster*	Jerry Remy
Boston Red Sox	A Season with *Wally The Green Monster*	Jerry Remy
Colorado Rockies	Hello, *Dinger*!	Aimee Aryal
Detroit Tigers	Hello, *Paws*!	Aimee Aryal
New York Yankees	Let's Go, *Yankees*!	Yogi Berra
New York Yankees	*Yankees Town*	Aimee Aryal
New York Mets	Hello, *Mr. Met*!	Rusty Staub
New York Mets	*Mr. Met* and his Journey Through the Big Apple	Aimee Aryal
St. Louis Cardinals	Hello, *Fredbird*!	Ozzie Smith
Philadelphia Phillies	Hello, *Phillie Phanatic*!	Aimee Aryal
Chicago Cubs	Let's Go, *Cubs*!	Aimee Aryal
Chicago White Sox	Let's Go, *White Sox*!	Aimee Aryal
Cleveland Indians	Hello, *Slider*!	Bob Feller
Seattle Mariners	Hello, *Mariner Moose*!	Aimee Aryal
Washington Nationals	Hello, *Screech*!	Aimee Aryal
Milwaukee Brewers	Hello, *Bernie Brewer*!	Aimee Aryal

College

Alabama	Hello, Big Al!	Aimee Aryal
Alabama	Roll Tide!	Ken Stabler
Alabama	Big Al's Journey Through the Yellowhammer State	Aimee Aryal
Arizona	Hello, Wilbur!	Lute Olson
Arkansas	Hello, Big Red!	Aimee Aryal
Arkansas	Big Red's Journey Through the Razorback State	Aimee Aryal
Auburn	Hello, Aubie!	Aimee Aryal
Auburn	War Eagle!	Pat Dye
Auburn	Aubie's Journey Through the Yellowhammer State	Aimee Aryal
Boston College	Hello, Baldwin!	Aimee Aryal
Brigham Young	Hello, Cosmo!	LaVell Edwards
Cal - Berkeley	Hello, Oski!	Aimee Aryal
Clemson	Hello, Tiger!	Aimee Aryal
Clemson	Tiger's Journey Through the Palmetto State	Aimee Aryal
Colorado	Hello, Ralphie!	Aimee Aryal
Connecticut	Hello, Jonathan!	Aimee Aryal
Duke	Hello, Blue Devil!	Aimee Aryal
Florida	Hello, Albert!	Aimee Aryal
Florida	Albert's Journey Through the Sunshine State	Aimee Aryal
Florida State	Let's Go, 'Noles!	Aimee Aryal
Georgia	Hello, Hairy Dawg!	Aimee Aryal
Georgia	How 'Bout Them Dawgs!	Vince Dooley
Georgia	Hairy Dawg's Journey Through the Peach State	Vince Dooley
Georgia Tech	Hello, Buzz!	Aimee Aryal
Gonzaga	Spike, The Gonzaga Bulldog	Mike Pringle
Illinois	Let's Go, Illini!	Aimee Aryal
Indiana	Let's Go, Hoosiers!	Aimee Aryal
Iowa	Hello, Herky!	Aimee Aryal
Iowa State	Hello, Cy!	Amy DeLashmutt
James Madison	Hello, Duke Dog!	Aimee Aryal
Kansas	Hello, Big Jay!	Aimee Aryal
Kansas State	Hello, Willie!	Dan Walter
Kentucky	Hello, Wildcat!	Aimee Aryal
LSU	Hello, Mike!	Aimee Aryal
LSU	Mike's Journey Through the Bayou State	Aimee Aryal
Maryland	Hello, Testudo!	Aimee Aryal
Michigan	Let's Go, Blue!	Aimee Aryal
Michigan State	Hello, Sparty!	Aimee Aryal
Minnesota	Hello, Goldy!	Aimee Aryal
Mississippi	Hello, Colonel Rebel!	Aimee Aryal

Pro Football

Carolina Panthers	Let's Go, Panthers!	Aimee Aryal
Chicago Bears	Let's Go, Bears!	Aimee Aryal
Dallas Cowboys	How 'Bout Them Cowboys!	Aimee Aryal
Green Bay Packers	Go, Pack, Go!	Aimee Aryal
Kansas City Chiefs	Let's Go, Chiefs!	Aimee Aryal
Minnesota Vikings	Let's Go, Vikings!	Aimee Aryal
New York Giants	Let's Go, Giants!	Aimee Aryal
New York Jets	J-E-T-S! Jets, Jets, Jets!	Aimee Aryal
New England Patriots	Let's Go, Patriots!	Aimee Aryal
Seattle Seahawks	Let's Go, Seahawks!	Aimee Aryal
Washington Redskins	Hail To The Redskins!	Aimee Aryal

Basketball

Dallas Mavericks	Let's Go, Mavs!	Mark Cuban
Boston Celtics	Let's Go, Celtics!	Aimee Aryal

Other

Kentucky Derby	White Diamond Runs For The Roses	Aimee Aryal
Marine Corps Marathon	Run, Miles, Run!	Aimee Aryal
Mississippi State	Hello, Bully!	Aimee Aryal
Missouri	Hello, Truman!	Todd Donoho
Nebraska	Hello, Herbie Husker!	Aimee Aryal
North Carolina	Hello, Rameses!	Aimee Aryal
North Carolina	Rameses' Journey Through the Tar Heel State	Aimee Aryal
North Carolina St.	Hello, Mr. Wuf!	Aimee Aryal
North Carolina St.	Mr. Wuf's Journey Through North Carolina	Aimee Aryal
Notre Dame	Let's Go, Irish!	Aimee Aryal
Ohio State	Hello, Brutus!	Aimee Aryal
Ohio State	Brutus' Journey	Aimee Aryal
Oklahoma	Let's Go, Sooners!	Aimee Aryal
Oklahoma State	Hello, Pistol Pete!	Aimee Aryal
Oregon	Go Ducks!	Aimee Aryal
Oregon State	Hello, Benny the Beaver!	Aimee Aryal
Penn State	Hello, Nittany Lion!	Aimee Aryal
Penn State	We Are Penn State!	Joe Paterno
Purdue	Hello, Purdue Pete!	Aimee Aryal
Rutgers	Hello, Scarlet Knight!	Aimee Aryal
South Carolina	Hello, Cocky!	Aimee Aryal
South Carolina	Cocky's Journey Through the Palmetto State	Aimee Aryal
So. California	Hello, Tommy Trojan!	Aimee Aryal
Syracuse	Hello, Otto!	Aimee Aryal
Tennessee	Hello, Smokey!	Aimee Aryal
Tennessee	Smokey's Journey Through the Volunteer State	Aimee Aryal
Texas	Hello, Hook 'Em!	Aimee Aryal
Texas	Hook 'Em's Journey Through the Lone Star State	Aimee Aryal
Texas A & M	Howdy, Reveille!	Aimee Aryal
Texas A & M	Reveille's Journey Through the Lone Star State	Aimee Aryal
Texas Tech	Hello, Masked Rider!	Aimee Aryal
UCLA	Hello, Joe Bruin!	Aimee Aryal
Virginia	Hello, CavMan!	Aimee Aryal
Virginia Tech	Hello, Hokie Bird!	Aimee Aryal
Virginia Tech	Yea, It's Hokie Game Day!	Frank Beamer
Virginia Tech	Hokie Bird's Journey Through Virginia	Aimee Aryal
Wake Forest	Hello, Demon Deacon!	Aimee Aryal
Washington	Hello, Harry the Husky!	Aimee Aryal
Washington State	Hello, Butch!	Aimee Aryal
West Virginia	Hello, Mountaineer!	Aimee Aryal
Wisconsin	Hello, Bucky!	Aimee Aryal
Wisconsin	Bucky's Journey Through the Badger State	Aimee Aryal

Order online at **mascotbooks.com** using promo code " **free**" to receive **FREE SHIPPING**!

More great titles coming soon!

info@mascotbooks.com